Trouble Is My Beeswax

Chet Gecko Mysteries

The Chameleon Wore Chartreuse
The Mystery of Mr. Nice
Farewell, My Lunchbag
The Big Nap
The Hamster of the Baskervilles
This Gum for Hire
The Malted Falcon
Trouble Is My Beeswax

And coming soon

Give My Regrets to Broadway
Murder, My Tweet

Trouble Is
My Beeswax

FROM THE TATTERED CASEBOOK OF

CHET GECKO
PRIVATE EYE

Bruce Hale

HARCOURT, INC.

Orlando • Austin • New York • San Diego • Toronto • London

Requests for permission to make copies of any part of the
work should be mailed to the following address:
Permissions Department, Harcourt, Inc.,
6277 Sea Harbor Drive, Orlando, Florida 32887-6777.

www.HarcourtBooks.com

Library of Congress Cataloging-in-Publication Data
Hale, Bruce.
Trouble is my beeswax: from the tattered casebook of
Chet Gecko, private eye/by Bruce Hale.
p. cm.
"A Chet Gecko Mystery."
Summary: Chet and his partner, Natalie Attired,
investigate a cheating ring at Emerson Hicky
Elementary school.
[1. Geckos—Fiction.   2. Animals—Fiction.
3. Schools—Fiction.   4. Cheating—Fiction.
5. Mystery and detective stories.   6. Humorous stories.]
I. Title.
PZ7.H1295Tr   2003
[Fic]—dc21   2003001105
ISBN 0-15-216718-8

Text set in Bembo
Display type set in Elroy
Designed by Ivan Holmes

First edition
A C E G H F D B

Printed in the United States of America

For my one and only Love Possum

A private message from the private eye . . .

Sooner or later, temptation knocks on everyone's door. Some of us throw the dead bolt, some ask it in and offer up a hot cup of cocoa—it all depends on your character. (Of course, as my mom likes to point out, *having* character isn't the same as *being* a character.)

Temptation has rapped plenty of times on my door—down at the end of Danger Street, around the corner from Trouble Avenue. Stenciled on the smoky glass you'll find: CHET GECKO, PRIVATE EYE. (Or you would, if I had a door with glass.)

Some say I'm the best detective at Emerson Hicky Elementary. I hate to argue when they're right.

Truth is, being a tough private eye, I can resist anything... except temptation. I can't say no to a silverfish sundae supreme; I've never met a cinnamon beetle crisp I didn't like. And when a mystery entices me, I dive right in and solve it.

But I draw the line when tempted to cheat.

Not everyone does, of course. This one time, I uncovered a cheating ring so underhanded, so successful, it exploded the myth that "cheaters never prosper." These crooks were so clever, they made Sherlock Holmes look like Elmer Fudd.

They led me on a wild-goose chase longer than an anaconda's suspenders. I got so discouraged, I almost gave up. But when tempted to surrender, I always recall my grandpa's words of wisdom: "If quitters never win and winners never quit, who came up with the saying 'Quit while you're ahead'?"

1

Cheat, Stink, and Be Hairy

It was no use, no use. I had followed a lead as thin as a dragonfly wafer until it finally petered out here, in a blind alley. Swiveling my head right and left, I could tell—

I was trapped. A whisper of fear tickled my neck. Then it hit me—*foom!* A shapeless something, heavier than a heartache, dropped onto my head and shoulders, dragging me down...down...when—

"Chet Gecko?" A voice cut through the red darkness.

"Are you with us?" said my teacher, Mr. Ratnose.

What was he *doing in the alley?*

My eyes blinked open. "Wuzza?" With a supreme effort, I raised my head.

"If you can't stay awake, I'll have someone pinch you," he said.

Several voices tittered.

Mr. Ratnose's classroom swam into focus. Kids, chairs, chalkboards, and cream cheese—Bo Newt grinning, Shirley Chameleon simpering. I was back at my desk, at school, facing down Public School Enemy Number One: boredom.

It was a humdrum morning at Emerson Hicky Elementary. You ask yourself, *How dull can it get?* Then you go to Mr. Ratnose's class, and you find out.

The school newspaper on the corkboard said it all: BOREDOM EPIDEMIC FLATTENS SCHOOL. No *duh*.

Mr. Ratnose shot me one last glare, then scrawled some numbers on the board. He claimed to be explaining fractions, but he might just as well have been describing his vacation in Left Armpit, Arizona.

I longed for something, anything, to break the monotony.

He turned with a flourish. "And now, time for history."

Anything but that.

But the lean rat had a surprise in store. He grabbed a stack of papers with one hand and *thwacked* them against his open palm.

"They say, 'History repeats itself,'" said Mr. Rat-nose. "But I sincerely hope yesterday's won't."

Bewildered faces greeted his remark.

Mr. Ratnose began pacing. "I'm referring, of course, to your grades on yesterday's history test. I am deeply disappointed in you."

Igor Beaver, a teacher's pet's pet, raised his hand. "Wh-what do you mean, teacher?" he whined. "Did I get a bad grade?"

Mr. Ratnose's whiskers bristled. "No, Igor," he said, keeping his voice even. "You got a good grade. In fact, *far too many* of you got a good grade."

Igor gasped. "You mean...?"

"I do. We've got cheaters!" Mr. Ratnose waved the stack of papers.

"B-but how do you know?" asked Igor.

"Because," our teacher snarled, "I added a dummy question."

I thought, *Giving a dummy question to these dummies is like sending snow to Eskimos.* But I didn't say it.

Mr. Ratnose looked like he was ready to take a bite out of our tests. "It was a trick question—none of you could've known the answer. But too many of you did."

He tossed the offending tests onto his desk. His gaze raked the classroom. "Look at the student on your right."

3

Igor and Cassandra the Stool Pigeon looked right. The rest of us stared at our teacher, beaming confusion like a country-western station beams corniness.

"*Look right!*" snarled Mr. Ratnose.

We looked.

"Now look left."

We looked again.

Mr. Ratnose bared his yellowy teeth. "One out of three of you is a cheater."

Cassandra raised her wing tip. "You mean, one-third of the class?"

Say what you will about the dame, she understood fractions.

"Exactly," said Mr. Ratnose. "And do you know what this means?"

Several students shook their heads.

"You're all taking the test again—right now."

The groan that followed could've been heard as far as Zanzibar. Given a choice between boredom and torture, I'll take boredom any day.

But we had no choice.

Igor and two other kids passed out the tests. I scanned mine. It was the same one we took yesterday.

And I didn't remember any more answers than I had the first time. While we sweated through multiple-choice madness, Mr. Ratnose patrolled the aisles, hairless pink tail dragging behind him.

Suddenly, he stopped. *"Hmm?"*

Mr. Ratnose bent and plucked a sheet of paper from the floor, beside Shirley Chameleon's desk. His forehead furrowed like a mole's front yard.

"Miss Chameleon, what is the meaning of this?" he said.

"Of what?" she asked. Shirley watched our teacher with one eye, while the other one shot me a worried glance. It's gross, but you get that from chameleons.

Brandishing the paper, Mr. Ratnose leaned over her. *"This,* as if you didn't know, is the answer key to the test!"

"No!" said Shirley.

"Oh, *yes,*" said Mr. Ratnose. "You, missy, are a dirty rotten cheater. One week of detention for you!"

Shirley crumpled like a paper pagoda in a rainstorm. Her eyes teared up.

That did it. I can't stand to see a reptile cry.

"Uh, Mr. Ratnose," I said, "let's not be hasty."

He turned his laser-beam gaze on me. "How's that?"

"I mean, how do you know it's Shirley's paper? She's never cheated before."

Mr. Ratnose's expression turned colder than a snow-snake's belly button. "Do you want to share her detention?" he asked.

"Um, no . . ."

"Then put a lid on it, mister." Mr. Ratnose turned to the class. "Everyone, back to your tests." He stalked off down the aisle.

Shirley swung her sorrowful puss in my direction. Her eyes held a plea. Her mouth framed a question. "Help me?" she whispered.

I nodded. After all, what self-respecting private eye would turn down a dame in distress?

A smart one, as I soon discovered.

2

Shirley, You Jest

Lunchtime came, as lunchtime will. I shouldered my way through the press of kids at the door, bent on sampling the marvels of our cafeteria. According to the menu, today's casserole would be drizzled with fungus gnat sauce, and a side order of—

Someone tugged at my sleeve.

"Um, Chet?" said Shirley Chameleon.

Oh, yeah. My client.

She looked as downtrodden as the doormat at an elephant's housewarming party. Shirley wrung her hands.

"What's the story, morning glory?" I said, leading her outside.

Shirley's cheeks glistened with tears, and her tail curled in a sad spiral. She was the kind of girl I could fall for—if someone pushed me from a great height.

Shirley trailed after me as I strolled down the hall. "Thanks for standing up for me," she said.

I shrugged.

"Chet, I didn't cheat. Please believe me."

"Doesn't matter what *I* believe, green eyes," I said. "Tell it to Old Man Ratnose."

"But can't you find some evidence to help me convince him?"

I looked her over. "Maybe. If you *are* innocent..."

"Why, Chet Gecko!" she said. "You know I'm not a cheater."

She was right. But that didn't mean I'd miss a chance to make her sweat.

"Swear it," I said.

"Cross my heart," said Shirley. Her fingers followed her words.

"Swear by something serious."

She frowned. "I swear by all that's chocolate."

"That's serious," I said, raising my eyebrows. "What else?"

Shirley eyed me for a few seconds. "I swear by the stack of Katydid Chunk bars I'll give you if you clear my name."

That's the kind of swearing I'd been waiting to hear.

"Good enough for me," I said. "Dry your eyes, señorita. You just bought yourself a detective."

As I savored my grub-'n'-tater casserole, I mulled over Shirley's problem. She swore she had no enemies, but somebody had either framed her or dropped his own cheat sheet.

The obvious suspects were the kids on the aisle where Mr. Ratnose had found the paper. I squinted, picturing the seating layout. Moving clockwise, we had: Cassandra the Stool Pigeon behind Shirley, then Jackdaw Ripper, Olive Drabb in front of Jack, and finally, two new kids—one in front of Olive, the other in front of Shirley.

I mopped my plate with a butterfly biscuit and considered my classmates. Being the type of gecko who thinks better on his feet, I tossed my tray on the dirty stack, popped the biscuit into my fly trap, and wandered around the lunchroom.

Two tables of kids had broken into pandemonium over trading cards. Three bullfrogs were conducting a belching contest. And five blue jays chased a crow down the table, weaving through other kids' trays like an obstacle course.

Pretty quiet for a Tuesday.

Cassandra stood by the door, shooting off her mouth to the lunch monitor. Drifting closer, I got an earful.

"... And then, Tiffany kept making this gross face until Brandon cracked up?" she said. "And he spewed his casserole all over me and the girl next to me? I swear, it was so sick. Can't you do something about it?"

Hmm. Cassandra was such a tattletale, she'd even rat on herself. Scratch suspect number one.

I moved on.

All alone on a bench by the wall, Olive Drabb huddled over her tray. She was a dun-colored field mouse with all the charm and personality of a sawdust-and-liverwurst sandwich. But Olive made up for it with a voice that inspired massive dozing.

"Hey, Olive," I said.

"*Mm,* hi," said Olive.

I leaned against the wall and eyeballed her. "Pretty rough, what happened to Shirley during the test," I said.

"I dunno," droned Olive. "Cheaters never prosper, don't ya know. Don't do the crime if ya can't do the time, is what I always say ..."

She probably said something else, but an unplanned nap attack made me miss it. My head jerked. I forced my eyes open and tried again.

"So, uh...do you get along with Shirley?"

The mouse nibbled a biscuit. "A friend in need is a friend indeed. You know, the eyes are the windows to the soul, but if you ask me, her eyes are kinda shifty, the way they..."

Once more, I zoned out. It seemed the only cliché she'd missed was the one she most needed to learn: Silence is golden.

I rubbed my eyes. "Um, that's fascinating," I said. "Listen, I gotta go now, but will you do me a favor?"

"What's that?"

"On the way home from school, don't talk to the bus driver."

3

Jackdaw Ripper

The minutes were tearing through my lunch period like an avalanche through a wet paper towel. Time flies when you're out of class.

I had just enough lunchtime left to squeeze in another interview before Mr. Ratnose's prison gates clanged shut again.

The cafeteria was nearly empty. I scooted out the door to track down my third suspect, Jackdaw Ripper. This lunch period, I'd saved the worst for last.

The din of students at play echoed across the grounds. As I watched, a touch-football game went from touch to shove, to slap, to *"You dirty little—"* Then a teacher stepped in.

Girls swarmed over the jungle gym. (You wouldn't

catch me on it until the thing had been seriously disinfected.)

Around me swirled rabbits and robins, rats and reptiles—but no Ripper. I chewed my lip. Remembering that the junior thugs liked to hang out by the bike racks in their spare time, I started in that direction.

Then, from the corner of my eye, I glimpsed movement. Something swooped down from the skies.

I hit the deck. *"Oof!"*

A dapper mockingbird landed beside me. "Call me crazy, but I think a pool might improve that swan dive," said my partner, Natalie Attired.

"You're crazy," I said.

She smirked and preened her wing feathers, "Sorry," she said, but wasn't.

Natalie Attired was my right-hand bird, a true-blue friend with a truly awful sense of humor. If she'd cracked as many cases as jokes, we'd be in the detective Hall of Fame.

"Chet, will you answer me something?"

"Shoot." I got to my feet and brushed off my shirtfront.

"Why didn't the elephant cross the road?" she asked.

I sighed. "Okay, why didn't he?"

"Because he didn't want to be mistaken for a chicken." She cackled.

See what I mean?

"Har-de-har," I said. "Now, bring your brain along. There's a case heating up, and it's time to do some grilling."

I filled her in as we trotted over to the bike racks. Sure enough, Jack Ripper was in a trio of toughs leaning on the racks, practicing their scowls. A delinquent horned toad named Rocky Rhode and a sullen ferret called Bosco Rebbizi flanked him.

Jackdaw Ripper was a magpie with attitude. His strong beak curved, cruel as a samurai sword, and his ebony eyes could count the change in your pocket from ten feet away on a dark night.

We stopped just out of reach. "Hey, sports fans," I said. "What's cookin'?"

"My fist and your face," snarled Rocky.

Bosco leaned toward her and muttered, "I think that's the answer to 'Got a match?'"

"But we're s'posed to threaten him," Rocky hissed.

"Yeah...," said Bosco. "But if he says, 'What's cookin'?' you say, 'Your buns in my oven.'"

She sulked. "I knew that."

I coughed. "So, Jack," I said. "How about Shirley getting busted for cheating, huh?"

"How about it," he said flatly. Rocky's ears perked up. (Or they would have if they hadn't been just a couple of holes in her head.)

"Do you like Shirley?" I asked.

The magpie squawked a laugh. "Like her? She's a girl."

"So?" said Natalie. "We were wondering if she really cheated."

Jack cocked his head. "Why ask me?"

"You sit by her," I said. "Thought you might have seen something."

He regarded us both with an expression as hard to read as model-assembly instructions in Swahili. "Maybe I did, and maybe I didn't," he said. "But I ain't dumb enough to go shootin' off my mouth in front of a private eye."

"How 'bout if I turn my back?" I said.

"Beat feet," said Rocky. "Yer breathin' up all the air."

Jack scowled. His practice had really paid off—his whole face bunched up like a muscle-man's fist.

Rocky and Bosco pushed up to standing. Rocky's brawny shoulders flexed like two camels playing Twister under a sheet. Bosco growled.

Knowing when to hoof it is a vital skill for a detective. I detected that it was time to hoof it.

"Let's go, Natalie," I said. "If any of you fine

specimens has some information, you know where to find us."

"Yeah," said Bosco. "In serious trouble."

I gave them a parting sneer. "That's right, ace. Trouble is my middle name."

As we walked away, Natalie said, "I thought your middle name was Sergio."

"Aw, what's in a name, Natalie *Petunia*?" I said.

For once, she shut up.

4

Petty Note Junction

Is anything sadder than the sound of the last lunch bell? (Okay, maybe the crumple of an empty bag when you've eaten the last Bar-B-Q Weevil chip.)

Natalie and I followed the bell's command and shuffled back to class. But as we went, we puzzled.

"Did you notice Rocky perk up when we mentioned cheating?" said Natalie.

"Her favorite subject," I said. "And Jack seemed like he was hiding something."

"Wonder what?"

I pushed my hat back. "Wonder about this, while you're at it: If a swallow named Fred is flying south with a pound of birdseed, and a sparrow named Mathilda is flying north with a pound of rice, which one—"

Natalie shook her head. "I won't do your math homework for you."

I shrugged. "Fair enough. So, why would someone frame Shirley?"

"Oh, that's easy," said Natalie. She ticked off the reasons on her feathertips. "One, they want revenge. Two, they want to hide their own cheating..." She paused.

"And what's three?" I asked.

"It was just an accident."

I snorted. "My money's on number one or two."

"Why's that?" she asked.

"Every time I use number three with my mom, she doesn't buy it."

Back in class, Mr. Ratnose gave his nerves a rest by assigning silent reading. Under cover of *The Three Little Pigs: Bakin' with Bacon* cookbook, I scoped out my classmates. Most were actually reading—which probably surprised Mr. Ratnose.

I surveyed the kids near Shirley. Which one of them wanted revenge on her?

Cassandra kept glancing around—looking for nonreaders to tattle on, no doubt. Olive's nose was buried in her book, but two of the new kids, Rimshot Binkley and Noah Vail, seemed restless.

Jackdaw's eyes met mine when I looked his way. Those shiny black peepers held more mischief than a carful of sixth graders. It was too early for conclusions, but I knew who topped my list of suspects.

Bimp!

A folded-up wad of paper bounced off my book and onto my lap. I opened it. In Shirley's neat cursive, the note read: *So, what's up? Do you know who framed me yet?*

I scrawled underneath it: *Not yet. Can you think of anyone who's jealous of you or wants revenge?*

I refolded the paper and—*bink*—flicked it back onto Shirley's desk.

She read it, glanced my way, chewed her pencil, and wrote a response. But when Shirley sent the note back, she gave it too much spin. The folded paper ricocheted off my book and onto the floor— *ka-bim-pok!*

Mr. Ratnose looked up.

Quickly, I ducked behind my book, turned my head, and shot out my tongue. *Th-zip!* I pulled the note into my mouth.

"Chet Gecko?" said Mr. Ratnose. "Is there a problem?"

I straightened and shook my head. "Uh-uh."

"Are you sure?"

I nodded. "Mm-hmm. Goodth bookh," I mumbled around the paper.

Satisfied, he returned to his own reading. I fished

the soggy paper from my mouth, read Shirley's message, and almost gagged.

You mean someone's jealous that I'm your girlfriend?

"You're *not* my girlfriend!" I hissed.

She pouted.

"But don't worry," I muttered. "I'll keep working on your case anyway."

Shirley's long tail curled around the chair leg. "Thanks," she whispered. "Just let me know if there's anything I can do."

"There *is* one thing," I said, leaning closer.

"Name it." Her eyelashes fluttered like a kite tail in a Force 5 hurricane.

"Don't study for the next test. You've gotta look less like a cheater and more like a moron."

The chameleon's eyes went hard. "I'll just follow your example," she said, and turned back to her book.

Great. I wanted a client; I got a comedian.

5

Ratty or Not

Afternoon recess blew in like the scent of fresh-baked spittlebug cookies. I hooked up with Natalie in the hallway, and we kicked around our next move.

When Mr. Ratnose marched past, we followed.

"Hey, teacher," I said. "Can we talk?"

He checked his watch, then Natalie and me. "If this is about your last math quiz," he said, "you can forget it. I won't raise that grade for love or money."

Natalie smirked.

"You mistake me," I said.

"Not often," he said. "Now, what's your gripe? I've got yard duty."

"We wanted to ask about Shirley's test," said Natalie.

"Oh, that." Mr. Ratnose's lips clamped tighter than an elephant's Speedo. He headed for the playground.

I hustled after him. "It's just that we don't believe a dame—" Natalie glared at me. "I mean, a *girl* like Shirley could've cheated."

"Believe it," he said.

"But she swears she didn't do it," said Natalie. "Can't you give her a second chance?"

Mr. Ratnose looked daggers. "Cheaters don't get a second chance."

Hmm. He was as hard to crack as a concrete coconut. But still we had to try.

"I don't suppose you'd let us see that test key you think she dropped?" I asked.

Mr. Ratnose's ears twitched. "You don't suppose right," he said. "That's evidence."

Natalie and I exchanged a frustrated glance.

Mr. Ratnose strode onto the grassy expanse of playground, head swiveling, on the lookout for mischief makers. We had maybe one more chance before he shut us down for good.

"But how would she get the answers from you?" asked Natalie.

"She stole them from my desk, she sneaked them off my computer . . . what does it matter?" said Mr. Ratnose.

I tried a different tack. "Look, we think she

might have been framed, maybe by a cheater covering his own tracks. Can you at least say who else you suspect of cheating?"

He stopped and fixed me with a hard stare. "I'll say one thing," he said. "I don't suspect you, Chet Gecko."

I smiled. "Gee, thanks. Because of my high morals?"

"No," he said, "because of your low grade-point average. If you were cheating, you wouldn't be hanging by your fingertips onto a C-plus in history."

He wasn't funny. But he was accurate.

"Can't you tell me anything useful, Mr. Ratnose?" I asked.

He clapped a paw onto my shoulder. "Do your homework, study hard, and obey your parents."

Just then, a squawk rang out from a knot of kids nearby.

My teacher stormed off to solve the situation. "It's all fun and games until someone loses a tail," he muttered.

Natalie watched him go. "Well, he's sure Mr. Helpful."

"This is nothing," I said. "You should see him when we're reviewing for a test."

I scanned the playground. A pack of kids nearby was engaged in a spirited version of capture the flag (or full-contact tiddlywinks, I'm not sure which). But it didn't matter. Natalie and I had higher-stakes games to play.

"Let's roll," I said.

"Like a rock," she replied. As we strolled along, Natalie said, "Hey, that reminds me of a great joke I heard today . . ."

"It would."

"What rock group do you find in an alley?" asked Natalie.

I shook my head.

"The *Bowling Stones*! Get it?" She cackled.

"Partner, you should be in the movies."

"Really?" Natalie preened herself.

"Yup," I said. "And if I had three bucks, I'd send you there right now."

6

A Vail of a Tale

Recess rolled on. Hoping for enough time to grill some suspicious characters and still squeeze in some R and R, I made for the swings.

"Hey, Chet?" said Natalie. "Where are we going?"

"Hunting other suspects."

"I've got an idea," she said.

"Save it; if you ever get another, you could breed them, and maybe they'll have babies."

My insult bounced right off her. "You ever notice," she said, "how, most cases we get, the newcomer tends to be the culprit?"

"Yeah?"

"So, let's interrogate the newcomers."

I grinned. "My thoughts exactly." As we reached

the sandbox, I swept my arm out in welcome. "Meet Newcomers Number One and Two."

The six swings were in full . . . uh . . . swing. And there, waiting in line, stood the Vails, brother and sister.

The two mourning doves had been at Emerson Hicky for less than a month. In class, Noah Vail sat in front of Olive Drabb, while Lacey, his sister, sat another row over.

Saying they had different personalities was like saying Buckingham Palace was a nice house. True, as far as it went. But it didn't go far enough.

Lacey's pearl gray feathers shimmered like a czarina's best bathrobe, and her eyes shone like a brand-new bicycle in a shop window. She dripped glamour like a snail drips slime—smoothly and without a thought.

Noah, on the other hand, was more hawk than dove. Rumor was, he'd been held back a grade at his old school, for fighting, feuding, and general rowdiness. His feathers were frazzled and his gaze was wild—like a werewolf at moonrise.

At that moment, his gaze lit on us.

"Morning, doves," said Natalie, grinning.

"Gee, I never heard that before," snarled Noah. I didn't know a bird could snarl. "Got any others?"

"Well, actually—"

I cut Natalie off. "We just came by to say howdy-do and see how you're getting along."

Lacey beamed at me and rested a wing tip on my arm. Seeing her this close made me dizzy—a nice dizzy, like slurping a milk shake on a merry-go-round.

"Why, that is so nice of you to ask," she said. "Isn't it, Noah?" She shot him a glance.

"Uh, yeah," he said.

"Truthfully, we like Emerson Hicky just fine," said Lacey. "But it's hard sometimes, having new teachers, meeting new people. It can get so... lonely."

My heart went out to her. Poor little birdie; she just needed a friend.

Natalie cleared her throat. "Have either of you gotten to know Shirley Chameleon?"

"What's it to you?" said Noah.

"Now, now, sunshine," cooed Lacey to her brother. "You must excuse Noah," she said. "He's been having a hard time fitting in."

Noah's chest pumped up like a gimmicky sneaker. "Oh, sure, just blab my problems to *every-one!*" he cried. *"Poor Noah—too bad he's not perfect like his little sister!"*

"That's not what I meant," said Lacey.

"Whatever," said her brother. "I'm outta here;

see you in class." And with that, he flapped his wings and took off for the gym.

Lacey forced a chuckle. "He's been under a lot of pressure lately. We both have. My parents expect nothing but the best."

I patted her shoulder. "And I'm sure they get it—from you," I said.

Where did that *come from?*

Natalie made a face, and I took my hand off the dove. "Um, about Shirley...?" my partner asked.

Lacey smoothed a perfect wing feather. "Yes, she seems like a lovely girl. But I'm sorry to say I don't really know her. I'll tell you, though..."

"Yes?" I said.

She turned a thousand-watt smile on me. "She sure has some wonderful friends." The glamorous dove glided over to an empty swing and sat down. "Ta-ta."

I gave her a wave and stumbled away from the sandbox.

Natalie fell in beside me. "*Ta-ta,* you *wonderful* friend," she said, in a dead-on imitation of Lacey.

"Hey, don't mock the poor kid," I said. "She's just new, that's all."

"Yeah," said Natalie. "But she uses the *oldest* lines."

I led the way across the grass. "Well, I don't know about her brother, but at least we know *she's* not involved in framing Shirley."

Natalie cocked her head. "Are you cracked? Nobody's that perfect. I think we should keep both of them on the suspects list."

"Maybe yes, maybe no," I said. "But there's one thing we know for sure."

"What's that?"

R-r-r-ring! went the bell.

"It's time to go back to class."

7

Trick or Cheat

When the last bell ended the day, our classroom exploded like the stink bomb in the school toilet that time that I—well, never mind.

Kids flew out the door (the birds did, anyway), laughing and chatting.

With the most mournful stare this side of a first grader's bedtime, Shirley dragged herself off to detention. But her sadness was real.

I looked away. A half day of snooping, and we hadn't uncovered anything to prove Shirley's innocence.

I scanned the classroom for our other new-kid suspect, Rimshot Binkley, but he'd already hopped down some rabbit hole and pulled it in after himself.

So I did what any self-respecting detective would

have done in my shoes. I went home for snacks with Natalie.

The afternoon shouldn't be a total waste, right?

The next morning, I sat down at my desk and found we were front-page news. CHEATERS PROSPER AT EMERSON HICKY, screamed the headline in our school newspaper, *The Daily Tattletale.*

The article revealed that one-third of Mr. Ratnose's class had cheated on a history test. *Uh-oh.* I knew of at least one pointy-nosed teacher who wouldn't be crazy about that story leaking out.

Speak of the devil. Mr. Ratnose stalked into the room looking like Hurricane Ratty. His eyes were slits, and his teeth ground together like a pencil sharpener on overtime.

The room fell silent so fast it almost hurt itself.

"Class," he said. "I am very, very, very, very unhappy with you."

Only an oblivious teacher's pet like Igor Beaver would follow a comment like that with a question.

"You didn't like my book report?" he asked.

The storm struck. "*Hang* your book report!" snapped Mr. Ratnose. He took a shaky breath. "In grading tests yesterday, I found that many of you are *still cheating.* Have you no sense of decency? No respect?"

It didn't seem like a good time to point out that we'd never had any decency or respect. I stayed mum.

Mr. Ratnose's gaze swept the room like a machine gun in the kind of movie your parents won't let you watch. "You will retake that test *again*,"— this time, nobody dared to groan—"and again, with different questions each time, until I'm satisfied. Is...that...clear?"

Heads bobbed in agreement. Waldo the furball dared to raise his hand.

"Yes, Waldo?" said our teacher.

"Ur, what if—what if you're never satisfied?" he said.

Mr. Ratnose stood like an old-time gunslinger, with feet spread wide. "If I'm not satisfied," he said, "everyone takes summer school."

8

Rich as Rocky, Feller

"That's it!" I told Natalie at recess. "I'm solving this case and putting the cheaters out of business if it's the last thing I do."

We were crossing a patch of new grass while around us spring had its way with Emerson Hicky students. A sixth-grade skink danced hip-hop in the hallway. A pack of my classmates thundered past, making for the library. A kitten and raccoon huddled close on a nearby wall.

Yuck. Spring makes for strange playmates.

"You really think we can solve two cases at once?" asked Natalie. She fluffed her feathers.

"I don't care," I said. "I'm not going to summer school, and I'm not gonna retake that stupid test until I'm a grandpa gecko. So, any bright ideas?"

She tilted her head back and stroked her chin feathers. "Try wearing a hot-pink T-shirt."

"Birdie, I'm warning you . . ."

"Or . . . *hmm* . . . to catch a cheater, think like a cheater."

I smiled. "That's the smartest thing you've said all day. So if I were a cheater, where would I get the test answers in advance?"

Our eyes met. "Rocky Rhode," we said together.

We found the low-down horny toad tormenting a first grader over by the krangleberry bushes. If anyone was selling stolen test answers, chances were, Rocky would have her claw in the business.

She was the wrongdoer's one-stop shop.

Natalie and I decided to fake some shopping. As we approached, Rocky's victim was just handing over half his sack lunch to the spiky lizard.

"And next time, bring some candied carpenter ants," said Rocky.

"I don't eat ants," whined the first grader, a shrimpy vole.

"But I do," said Rocky. She thanked him for his generosity by punting the little guy halfway to the basketball courts. Then she turned to Natalie and me.

"Wanna ride?" She sneered.

I coughed. "Maybe later. We're here on business."

"Monkey business?" Her eyes narrowed.

"The monkiest." Nat grinned.

"But can you mind your own beeswax?" asked Rocky.

"Trouble is my beeswax," I said.

"So it's no trouble to mind it," added Natalie.

Rocky frowned. We were moving a little too fast for her. Time to spell things out.

"We're in the market for some test answers," I mumbled.

Rocky Rhode eyeballed the two of us. We tried to look dishonest.

She stroked her jaw while suspicion wrestled with greed. Greed won. Rocky shifted from bully to businessperson.

"Whaddaya want?" she said, opening a book bag to flash a sheaf of papers. "I got quizzes; I got tests; I got true-false; I got multiple-choice." She leaned closer. "Essays cost extra."

"How is the multiple-choice?" asked Natalie.

"It's choice," said Rocky.

I leaned closer. "Have you got the answers for Mr. Ratnose's history quiz—the one he's giving today?"

"What are ya, cracked?" said Rocky. She pushed my shoulder like a pile driver.

"Some think so," said Natalie.

"I can't get answers for a same-day test—it's too quick," said the massive horned toad. "Only way to get those answers is to copy off some brainiac's paper."

I rubbed my shoulder. "But lots of kids have been cheating in my class—not by copying, 'cause I've checked. Didn't you sell answers to some of them?"

"I can't say," said Rocky. She pretend-zipped her lips. "Professional ethics."

"Professional ethics?" I said. "You're selling test answers!"

"Even so," said the horned toad.

Natalie stepped forward. "Chet's class took a test yesterday, and a bunch of kids cheated. If you didn't supply the answers, someone did."

A cloud passed over Rocky's lumpy features. Her fists tightened.

"Yeah, *someone* did," she said. "And when I get my paws on that someone, they're gonna wish they . . . they'd never been born."

"Or hatched," said Natalie helpfully.

"Or hatched . . . ," said Rocky.

"Or foaled."

Rocky pointed a clawed finger at my partner. "Don't push it."

"So," I said, tilting back my hat, "big bad Rocky can't handle a little competition?"

"Can so," growled the horned toad. She took a threatening step closer.

Natalie and I backpedaled.

My partner held up her wings. "Whoa, Nellie," said Natalie. "We're just saying, it'd be a shame if some newcomer put you out of business. You're like . . . an institution."

Rocky let her shoulders slump. "Ain't it the truth. But my customers got no respect for tradition. They're going to this new kid, with his newfangled ways."

"What do you mean?" I asked.

Rocky looked bluer than a click beetle on ice. "I heard he's got some high-tech way of stealing the answers." She stared into her book bag. "Why don't he just break into desks, or sell last year's tests, like we always done?"

I elbowed Natalie. We left the mournful sixth grader with her memories and pointed our toes toward class.

The bell rang. Kids began flowing off the playground like dirty bathwater sluicing down the drain. I noticed, over by the basketball courts, Jackdaw Ripper in deep conversation with a burly raccoon.

"Hey, Natalie, who's the shifty-looking guy with Jack?" I asked.

She looked over. "I dunno. Some raccoon—they always look shifty."

"Must be the mask," I said.

We walked in silence awhile.

Natalie spoke up. "So, Mr. Private Eye? What do you think?"

"I think they oughta just give up and put chocolate milk in the drinking fountains, already," I said.

"About our case, ding-a-ling," said Natalie.

"I'm not sure. So far, we've got some unknown kid selling test answers..."

"Which he steals from teachers..."

"Using some unknown high-tech method," I said. "Oh, and we've also got someone framing Shirley for reasons unknown. We don't know much."

Natalie clapped me on the shoulder. "They say ignorance is bliss," she said.

I sighed and stepped into my classroom. "If that's true, birdie, we should be the happiest mugs on campus."

9

E-Mail & Female

Usually, computer lab is the bright spot in an otherwise drab day. (Or it *was,* until they found the games we'd sneaked onto the machines. Why Principal Zero doesn't consider *Tiki Taki Boom* educational material, I'll never know.)

That morning, Mr. Ratnose packed us off for a half hour of computer time. We spent it under the supervision of Cool Beans, our librarian, media guy, and local expert on the supernatural. (The big possum also blows a mean kazoo, but that's neither here nor there.)

When my turn came on the computer, I logged in, pulled up my book project, and started to work. It was a literary masterpiece designed to rescue my English grade. I called it *Pat the Bunny Meets King Kong.*

But before I could type more than a sentence, the computer made a soft *poot*. Digital farts? I looked closer at the screen.

There, in the corner, a blinking envelope announced, *"Instant Mail!"* Mail for me? I clicked on the envelope. The message opened:

Chasing cheaters?
Need a clue?
Don't forget about computers!!! :-)

I looked up from the screen and scanned the room.

My classmates were working on their projects, playing games, or making rude faces at each other. At one table, a couple of kids from the school paper,

a blue jay and a kitten, typed on their own computers. Cool Beans patrolled the aisle, slow as a molasses landslide.

Nobody gave me a sneaky wink or knowing nod.

No way to tell who'd sent the message. The return address said only *FooFoo*.

I typed a reply:

Foo—
Huh?
What about computers?

In less than a minute, I had my answer, if you could call it that:

Do I gotta spell it out?
Okay. Here's a hint:
What kind of web doesn't catch flies?

That was all. I sent several more messages, but no reply came. My mysterious informant kept mum.

Finally, when I was ready to toss in the towel, the computer went *poot!* Another blinking envelope appeared. This message read:

Gecko—
Keep your beak outta things what don't concern you.
Lay off, or else!!!!!

No signature, but the return address was *Stinky-UnderWare*. A survey of the room revealed no scowling bad guys or, for that matter, stinkers, either. Even Jackdaw Ripper was busy with his project.

Was this some kind of prank?

My brooding was cut short by Mr. Ratnose, who rounded us up and marched us off to class. My body went, but my mind stayed behind. *Who are FooFoo and Stinky?* I wondered, and, *What's all this about flies?*

Mmm, flies. Thinking about them made my stomach rumble.

Shirley had promised some Katydid Chunk bars if I cleared her name. But right now, the chance of enjoying them seemed as remote as a restroom on Pluto—too far away to count on.

My stomach pouted. We dragged into class and sat down.

This time, Mr. Ratnose had a surprise. He'd imported some parents as monitors. They quickly passed out the tests and began roaming the aisles with sour expressions.

"Just remember," said Mr. Ratnose. "I can keep this up as long as you can. If you want to spend your summer in this room, just cheat on your science test tomorrow. I love summer school."

The idea of spending summer watching Mr. Ratnose in Bermuda shorts was too scary for words. I hoped my classmates would cool it. But a good detective knows animal nature. I braced for the worst.

As the test began, I was determined to spot the cheater near Shirley. Throughout the exam, I kept sneaking peeks at her neighbors: Jack, Cassandra, Olive, Noah, and Rimshot. I could've used a third eye to watch for Mr. Ratnose and the parents, but geckos only come with two.

At last, my snooping paid off. Rimshot Binkley, the edgy rabbit, kept glancing down to his right before writing his answers.

Ah-ha!

From my angle, I couldn't tell what he was looking at, but it had to be the test answers. I leaned over my desk, craning to see . . .

"Chet Gecko," hissed Mr. Ratnose. "Eyes on your own paper!" He stiff-armed me back into my seat.

"Just stretching, Mr. Ratnose," I whispered.

He snorted. "Stretching the truth is more like it."

I settled back into test-taking with an easy mind. Rimshot Binkley was in my sights. I had a break at last, and before too long, that rabbit would sing like a silver-tongued thrush at a karaoke club.

A smile tugged at my lips. *Katydid Chunk bars, here I come.*

10

Rimshot Binkley

By the time the test ended, Mr. Ratnose's nerves were shot. I could tell because he gave us quiet reading until lunch, and it wasn't even quiet-reading time.

But I didn't care. It let me check out my cheater. I swapped seats with Bo Newt, in front of me, to get a better gander at Rimshot Binkley.

The rabbit looked shiftier than a sackful of jumping beans. His nose twitched like sow-bug sushi; his sunken eyes were black as raisins and his cheeks puffy as potato-bug muffins. (Or maybe I was just ready for lunch.)

Binkley hunched over his book but did a poor job faking reading. His eyes jittered around the classroom, and his book was upside down.

When the lunch bell rang, I slipped out the door behind him. We rounded the corner, and I snagged his elbow.

"Heya, slick," I said. "How'd you do on that test?"

The rabbit's raisin eyes nearly popped from his head. "T-t-test?" he stuttered. "Wh-what do you mean?"

I gripped his arm and steered him around the side of the building, out of sight. Rimshot Binkley started shaking like doodlebug Jell-O.

"Come on, you can tell me," I said. "I know you had some kind of system going. What, did you write the answers on your arm?"

"A-a-arm?"

I pushed up his jacket sleeve, but the right arm was empty, except for his watch. "Is it in your pocket?" Fishing in his pocket yielded nothing but lint and the stub of a moldy carrot.

"I d-don't know wh-what you're—"

"Cut the hip-hop, Bugsy," I said. "I saw you cheat." Grabbing the rabbit by his jacket, I shoved him against the wall. "Spill the beans or—"

"All right, all right!" Binkley held up his paws. "I'll spill."

I kept a loose hold on the jacket, in case his feet got itchy. "I'm listening."

Rimshot Binkley's chin sunk onto his gray-furred chest. "I cheated," he whispered. "Please, d-don't tell."

I felt sorry for the guy, he looked so whipped. But I put my sympathy on hold—I had a case to crack.

"I might not rat you out," I said, "*if* you tell me what I need to know."

His head rose, and his eyes went wide. "Anything!"

"Why'd you do it?" I said.

Binkley bit his lip.

"Well, I'm new at school, and the classwork is so hard..."

"No, cabbage-head, *why* did you frame Shirley?"

"Wh-what?" he said. "Who's Shirley?"

I tightened my grip and shook him. "Can the charade. You dropped your answer sheet and let her take the rap for cheating. Why?"

The rabbit's nose wiggled like a worm trying to escape the early bird.

"I d-didn't do that," said Binkley. "I swear!"

"Come on..."

"Really. I d-didn't even use an answer sheet." He glanced nervously at his watch.

"Come clean," I said, grabbing his arm. "The answers to this test aren't on your watch, buddy boy."

He blinked. "You're right. It's got the answers to tomorrow's quiz."

"Huh?" I took a closer look at the wristwatch.

Rimshot Binkley pressed a button, and the digital display changed from the time to a sequence of numbers and letters—1C, 2A, 3A. He touched another button, and the display scrolled, giving test answers up to question twenty.

Twenty questions, twenty answers. I had to admit it was pretty slick.

"I'll g-give it to you," he said, slipping off the watch. "Just d-don't tell."

I released the rabbit's arm. "So, if you didn't frame Shirley," I said, half to myself, "who did?"

Rimshot Binkley shrugged, holding the timepiece out to me.

I'd be lying to say I wasn't tempted. But Mrs. Gecko didn't raise no cheaters. (Language manglers, maybe.)

I pushed his hand back. "Where'd you get this gizmo?" I asked.

He clasped the watch to his chest and jumped. "N-no, I can't tell!" he cried. "Stripes w-would skin me a-alive!"

And as I watched, the gray rabbit realized I wasn't holding him. His bunny legs did what bunny legs do: get hoppin'. And before you could say, "slow-witted detective," he was gone.

11

The Whole Kitten Caboodle

I had plenty of food for thought, but what I needed right then was the other kind. Making tracks for the cafeteria, I considered Binkley's reactions.

He'd been too scared to lie, probably. But if he was telling the truth, it opened up a whole new can of worms. And this gecko doesn't like worms—even the butterscotch kind.

Who was Stripes? Had he or she sold other watches to cheaters? And how did that tie in with Shirley's predicament? The questions chased through my noggin like alley cats after a wagon load of tuna-fish sandwiches.

I pushed my tray past the tubs of grub while Mrs. Bagoong and her lunch ladies piled my plate high.

Tuesday was chef's choice, and that meant pond-scum quiche. *Yum.*

But lunch didn't last. Before long, I'd cleaned my plate and was ready to move on to trickier fare: tracking down cheaters.

I stepped through the double doors and strolled alongside the building. Out across the grass, Jackdaw Ripper was weaving his sneaky way between groups of kids. I leaned on the railing to watch.

A voice broke my concentration. "You're Chet Gecko?" someone purred.

"If I can trust what my mom tells me," I said. I swiveled my head.

A kitten stretched luxuriously and leaned on the railing beside me. "I hear Old Man Ratnose made you guys take that test over. Twice."

"Yeah. So?"

I checked her out. The kitty's ginger-striped fur was fluffier than a cloud soufflé, and it shone like moonlight in a glass of milk. *She must spend a fortune on conditioner,* I thought.

"I hear it was because so many people cheated," she said.

"My, my, Grandma. What big ears you have."

"I've got twenty-twenty hearing, Mr. P.I." Her ears swiveled.

"And where'd you get your scoop?" I asked.

The kitten watched kids playing tag. "A little bird told me," she said.

Cassandra the Stool Pigeon, no doubt. That bird's mouth ran like a bully with a wedgie: fast and furious.

I turned toward the kitten and rested an elbow on the rail.

"Did you know that a couple of the sixth-grade teachers have also been having problems with cheaters?" she asked.

"No, but then I don't know how a Kickapoo gets his kicks, either," I said. "Why so many questions?"

The kitten straightened her whiskers. "It's my job to be nosy," she said.

"What, you're a principal?"

"No, silly, a journalist." She offered me her paw. "Kitten Caboodle, ace reporter for *The Daily Tattle-tale*."

Great. Just what I needed—a reporter sticking her snoot into my business.

"Well, whoop-de-doo and Kalamazoo," I said, ignoring her outstretched paw. "What's all this got to do with me?"

Kitten batted her mismatched eyes—one blue, one gold. "Come on," she said. "What kind of fool do you take me for?"

"First-class."

Her smile was as painted-on as a chocolate-milk mustache. "You're a detective," she purred. "And

Emerson Hicky has a cheating ring. It's obvious:
You're trying to bust it wide open."

"What?"

"Tell me," she said, pulling out a notepad. "What
progress have you made?"

I gritted my teeth. "None. I'm not on the case."

"Really? That's not what I heard."

"Maybe your hearing's only fifty-fifty."

She ignored me and scribbled on her pad. "I can
see the headline now," Kitten said, "'Cheating Ring
Baffles Detective.'"

I crossed my arms. "Look here, kitty cat. In the
first case, I'm *not* investigating a cheating ring. In

the second case, I'm not baffled. And in the third case..."

"Yes?"

"What does *baffled* mean, anyway?"

Kitten arched an eyebrow. "It's journalism talk," she said smugly.

"And this is private-eye talk," I said. "*Sayonara,* fuzz-ball." I pivoted on my heel and marched off to find Natalie.

"But—" she said.

"Gotta split, Kitten. People to go, places to meet..."

"Wait!" she called. "Don't you want to give me a comment?"

I had one, but my dad had washed my mouth out the last time I made it. A cheery wave would have to do.

I hustled across the playground. The reporter watched from the railing but made no move to follow.

My full belly appreciated it when I slowed to a trot. Pond-scum quiche does better when it's stirred, not shaken.

As expected, my partner was roosting on a low limb of the scrofulous tree, with eyes closed and a tiny string of drool trailing from the side of her beak.

"Rise and shine, Frankenstein," I said. "We're not gonna catch any cheaters with you catching Zs."

Natalie's eyes popped open. "Who's sleeping?" she yawned. "I was resting my eyes, waiting for you."

"Uh-huh."

The mockingbird spread her wings and floated to the ground. "I was just thinking," she said. "Do you know what happened to the survivors of a wreck involving a red ship and a blue ship?"

"What?"

"They were *maroon*ed!" She cackled. "Gotcha, hotshot."

I rubbed my forehead. "Do you *dream* in bad jokes, too?"

12

Ways & Beans

Before she could tell any more stinkers, I filled Natalie in on the latest events: Rimshot Binkley's confession, Kitten's news about other cheating classrooms, and my mysterious e-mail messages.

"Gee," she said, "you've been a busy lizard. Leave something for your partner, why don't you?"

"I did," I said. "Can't you figure out my e-mail clue from FooFoo?"

Natalie chuckled. "You mean the riddle, 'What kind of web doesn't catch flies?' That's too easy."

I put a hand on my hip. "Oh, yeah? Then, what's the answer?"

"A *Web* site," she said. "Don't you ever use a computer?"

"A Web site? I don't get it."

My partner started heading off the playground. I followed.

"Hello?" she said. "Computers? World Wide Web? Web site?"

"I know what a Web site is, worm-breath."

Natalie raised a wing feather. "Okay, what was that first message?" she said. "Something like, 'Wanna catch cheaters? Don't forget about computers,' right?"

"Right."

"So . . . somebody's using a Web site to cheat."

I scratched my head. "But how?"

"Beats me." She shrugged. "That's why we're asking the expert."

I looked up to find she'd led us to the doors of the library. Inside, we'd find the air-conditioned coolness of the computer lab, and the natural coolness of our media expert, Cool Beans.

"Quick thinking, partner," I said.

"And that ain't birdseed." She winked.

"Whatever."

Together we pushed through the heavy oak doors.

Chilly and crisp as a polar bear's pajamas, the library was lightly populated at lunchtime. A handful of kids pored over picture books at the low tables ahead of us. Off to the left, the computer lab stood nearly empty—just Lacey Vail, a bullfrog from Nat's class, and the queen of nosiness, Kitten Caboodle.

I grabbed Natalie and spun away from the lab. "That's her!" I hissed.

"Her who?"

"Kitten Caboodle, over by the computers. That snoop."

Natalie swiveled back to see.

"Don't—" I started.

"Well, well," a familiar voice purred. "Big-shot detective brings in his partner." Kitten grinned at us and licked a paw. "This case must be heating up."

I gave her my steely-eyed look. "For the last time, pencil-pusher, we're not investigating any cheaters."

"For your information," she said, "I use a computer to write my stories—not a pencil. And I've got a nose for news. You two are onto something."

Natalie flashed a smile. "Well, maybe your nose stinks," she said. "Chet and I are here to get help with our book reports."

The reporter looked from one of us to the other, frowning. She didn't quite buy our story, but she didn't know why.

"Later, tater," I said. "Schoolwork calls."

Natalie and I ambled back to the circulation desk of Cool Beans, an opossum in shades and a snappy blue beret. He nodded.

"Well, if it ain't the shamus and his sidekick," he rumbled. "What's shakin', green gumshoe?"

"Nothing but the knees of my teacher," I said. "We need your help with a little, um, research."

"I'm your possum."

Natalie jerked her head toward Kitten Caboodle. The ginger-striped cat was watching us, with ears poised like satellite dishes.

"Maybe we should talk somewhere else," said Natalie.

"Ankle on over to my private pad," said Cool Beans.

We followed as he moseyed slo-o-owly down a short hall to his office. I guess for a possum, that was hustling.

Once inside, he leaned on a battered desk stacked high with jazz CDs and magazines like *Young Were-wolf Quarterly* and *Modern Vampire*. Joe Normal he wasn't.

"What's the scoop, Betty Boop?" said Cool Beans. "Need my help investigatin' some evil super-natural power?"

"In a way," I said. I pushed back my hat. "What do you know about computers?"

In short order, the librarian had given us the low-down. Yes, the cheaters could be using a Web site, he explained. If someone posted test answers on the site, anyone with a password could download what they needed.

"But how are these computerized crooks getting the answers in the first place?" asked Natalie.

Cool Beans scratched under his beret. "I s'pose they're just liftin' 'em from the teachers," he said. "Wouldn't be too hard. You just break into the classroom all quietlike and heist the answer sheet. Or . . ."

"Yes?" I said.

"If they were *really* hip . . ."

"What?" said Natalie.

"They'd *hack*," said Cool Beans. He looked at us expectantly.

"Go ahead and spit if you need to," I said.

Natalie elbowed me. "No, bug-brain; he means they hack into the teacher's computer to get the answers."

I frowned at Cool Beans. "With an ax?"

"Negatory, daddy-o," he said. "With another computer."

"I see," I said. (Actually, I didn't.)

"Wait a minute," said Natalie. "I'm about to have a brainstorm!"

I shot her a look. "I'll fetch my umbrella."

Natalie glanced from me to Cool Beans. "Rocky Rhode told us some kid found a high-tech way to get test answers," she said.

"Right...," I said.

"What if that kid was hacking into the teachers' computers?"

I folded my arms. "Well...call me old-fashioned, but my money's on the tried-and-true breaking-and-entering method."

Natalie began to pace. "Either way, the thief could post the answers, then his customers could buy a password, right?"

"Righty-ro," said the librarian.

The lights came on in the attic of my brain. "Then kids like Rimshot could load the answers onto their fancy watches and cheat away!"

"Right under the teacher's nose," said Natalie.

I bit my lip. "There's only one thing..."

"Yes?" said Cool Beans.

"What the heck does all this have to do with framing Shirley for cheating?"

The big possum shrugged. "Search me, Sherlock," he said. "That's for *you* to decipher."

"I'll put it on my to-do list," I said.

Natalie and I thanked Cool Beans. We hustled through the library, out into the sunshine, without picking up any pesky reporters.

"That to-do list isn't too bad," said Natalie.

"Nah," I said. "All we've gotta do is figure out who framed Shirley, get 'em to confess, sort out who's running a cheating ring and how they're doing it, and shut 'em down."

"You forgot one thing," said Natalie.

"What?"

"Study for the history test, in case Mr. Ratnose makes you take it again."

Oh, yeah. Schoolwork. It sure does put a crimp in a private eye's day.

13

Goon with the Wind

Wouldn't you know it? Just before we could make our next move, lunchtime ran out like the last of the Halloween candy. It was back to the salt mines (also known as Mr. Ratnose's class).

Everyone seemed shell-shocked from the barrage of testing, including our teacher. He tottered through the science lesson like a robo rat running low on batteries. (Not that it mattered. That class was dull, no matter *how* he felt.)

When recess came, it was as welcome as a candied bee in a birthday cake. I hit the playground to resume our investigation. We needed a break, a lead, something to link our two cases—but I didn't know what.

Natalie and I climbed onto a low limb of the scrofulous tree to spy on the scene. From our perch, I spotted Bo and Tony Newt grappling like Antone "the Stone" Jones, a popular wrestler on TV.

Farther off, Lacey and Noah Vail were arguing by the tetherball courts, Olive Drabb was boring some poor kid to sleep, and Jackdaw Ripper—

"Natalie, check that out!" I pointed to where the magpie stood with a burly raccoon near the bushes. "That's the same coon he was with earlier."

She nodded. "Yeah, so?"

"What did Rimshot say when I asked him to tell where he got the answers?"

"Stripes would skin him alive," we said together.

Natalie grinned. "That guy's tail looks pretty stripy to me."

"Shall we?"

But by the time we'd scrambled down from the tree and hoofed it over to the bushes, Jack had pulled a vanishing act. Only his *compadre* stayed behind.

We approached the hefty coon with caution. Those things could bite. But we needn't have worried.

The raccoon was as fat and sassy as a kid who's locked himself in a candy store. A dark mask ringed mild, curious eyes, which crinkled in a smile as we drew closer. He beckoned to us with a paw smeared with brown chocolate. (At least, I hoped it was chocolate.)

"Don't be shy, friends," he said. "Right this way. Johnny Ringo's the name. And, well, I guess you know my game, or you wouldn't be here."

I told him our names.

"So, amigos, what'll it be?" he said, rubbing his paws together.

"Uh..." I looked at Natalie. Small detail. We hadn't discussed a plan.

"We, uh, were just curious," she said. "What were you talking about with Jackdaw?" The direct approach—simple but effective.

A slight wrinkle appeared between Johnny Ringo's eyebrows. "I'm afraid that comes under the heading of nunya."

"'Nunya'?" I asked.

"Nunya business," said Johnny Ringo. So much for the direct approach. "And speaking of businesses, I'm trying to run one here. If you're not going to buy anything, I suggest you move along."

I looked around. "Where's the merchandise?"

The raccoon squinted at us and gnawed his upper lip. "Not so fast," he said. "You could be stool pigeons. How do I know I can trust you?"

"Well," said Natalie, "first of all, I'm a mockingbird, not a pigeon..."

"Cute," said Johnny.

"And second of all," I said, "Rimshot Binkley sent us. He really liked the *watch* you sold him." I gave him a big wink.

Johnny's face shut down like a bank vault at closing time. He stuck two fingers in his mouth and whistled sharply.

Two identical wolverines, thick as fur-coated refrigerators, stepped out of the bushes. Menace rolled off them like waves at Waikiki, and their fang-filled smiles said, *Snack time, at last.*

"Wha—" I said, stumbling back.

"It's quite simple," said Johnny Ringo. "Only my sales representatives can make referrals, and Binkley is definitely *not* one of my reps."

Wolverine One growled, "Hey, boss. You want we should bloop these bozos?"

The raccoon rubbed his hands together. "Yes, I think a little blooping is in order. And when you finish with these two, visit that blabbermouth Binkley."

You didn't need to be a Psychic Friend to figure out that "blooping" would be bad for the health.

Johnny Ringo's two goons advanced.

I pointed behind them. "Great golliwogs! Is that Principal Zero?"

Only a moron would fall for an old trick like that. Fortunately, the two wolverines were morons. They looked.

Before Johnny could snarl, "Get them!" Natalie and I skedaddled. We raced across the playground, with the wolverines in hot pursuit.

"I think we hit a nerve there," Natalie puffed, as she flapped herself airborne.

"Really?" I said. "How could you tell?"

After that, we saved our breath for fleeing. The raccoon's muscle-heads chased us past the sandbox, through a tetherball game, down the halls, and out into the parking lot.

They would've chased us all the way to Tierra del Fuego, if Natalie and I hadn't hit on the bright idea of climbing the flagpole. As it was, they nearly shook us off it.

Only the ring of the bell and the actual arrival of Principal Zero stopped the wolverines' shenanigans. He grabbed each one by the scruff of the neck.

"Don't tell me; let me guess." The hefty tomcat addressed Natalie and me. "You were just minding your own business, when these two rascals started chasing you."

"Something like that," I said.

Principal Zero shook his head. "Gecko," he said, "the day you tell me the whole truth is the day I have kittens."

"*Cat*'ll be the day," said Natalie.

The principal groaned at her pun. For once, we saw eye to eye on something.

14

Shrink Rapped

The final period of the day lasted as long as the Roman Empire, but without all the old guys in bedsheets and olive leaves. The students sagged, the teacher slumped. Even the chalkboard looked bored.

Mr. Ratnose's whiskers drooped as he droned through a discussion of *Razzleberry Finn,* our assigned reading.

Try as I might, I couldn't keep my mind on ol' Razzleberry and his problems. I had my own worries—like sussing out who had gotten Shirley in trouble.

Sure, it looked like Johnny Ringo was behind the schoolwide cheating, but he had no beef with Shirley. That made it one of my double-dealing classmates, but which one?

I scratched my chin. It'd sure help if I knew more about a cheater's mind...

Then I had a bright idea. (It happens sometimes.)

I slapped a sad look onto my kisser and waited for Mr. Ratnose to notice. When he kept droning on, I heaved a sigh heavier than a hippo in a baby sling, then whimpered.

Mr. Ratnose eyed me. "What's up with you?" he said.

"Oh, nothing," I said. I bit the inside of my cheek, hard, and just like that, my eyes watered. (I'd road tested this technique at home.)

My teacher closed his book. "Is something wrong?"

I pinched the bridge of my nose, shook my head, and muttered, "The horror...the horror."

Mr. Ratnose walked over to me. He took my chin in his paw and raised my face. I maintained the woeful expression that usually worked when I needed a sick day.

"You seem awfully stressed out," he said. "Maybe you should visit the school counselor."

I played my trump card. "No, I don't want to be any trouble."

"Nonsense," he said. "You're going, and that's that." Mr. Ratnose scrawled on a hall pass and handed it to me.

Shoulders slumped, I dragged out the door. Shirley's worried gaze followed me, but I couldn't slip her a signal; Ratnose was watching.

Outside, I trucked down the halls with a happy whistle. If I played him right, the school counselor might give me some answers. And even if he didn't, I was out of class and fancy-free.

The counselor's office perched at the far end of the administration building. Small and stuffy, it was as full of books as an older brother is full of trickery.

I poked my head through the doorway.

"Ye-es?" came a quavery voice. "Was there something?"

Whip Van Wrinkle leaned on the desk, looking like a strong sneeze would blow him over. The network of creases covering this whiptail lizard looked like the root system of a redwood tree. Even his wrinkles had wrinkles.

But his eyes were sharper than the hidden pins in a store-bought dress shirt.

"Take a seat," he said.

I sat. "Listen, shrink, I'm on a case and I'm hoping you can help me."

"That's my job."

"Then tell me," I said, "what makes a cheater cheat?"

73

Mr. Van Wrinkle scratched the wattles under his chin. "A cheater, eh? Well, sonny-boy—"

"The name's Chet."

"Well, Jet, it's a complicated thing. Yessir. Kids cheat for many reasons."

I put my hands on my knees and leaned forward. "Such as?"

"Some students need approval, and some have parents who expect perfection," he said. "Some feel they can't keep up with schoolwork, while others . . ."

"Yes?" I said.

"Well, Jet—"

"That's *Chet.*"

"Just what I said, *Pet.* Other children have *flexible morals* and will exploit an opportunity." Whip Van Wrinkle's eyes bored into me like a mole into a dirt sandwich.

I shrugged. "What?"

"Tell me, why did you *really* come in here?"

"Like I said, I'm working a case."

He steepled his fingers, and his tail switched slowly. "Mm-*hmm.*"

"What does that mean?" I asked.

"It means . . . mm-*hmm,*" he said. "Have you ever thought, Pet—"

"That's—aw, never mind."

"... That perhaps you're investigating cheaters because you, yourself, want to cheat?"

"What?" I said, getting to my feet. "You're cracked!"

The old lizard waggled a finger. "That's *mentally unbalanced*. Now, tell the truth."

"I—I never..." My voice croaked, and my eyes went watery. *What was this?*

"Ye-e-es? Tell me all..." Mr. Van Wrinkle's voice soothed.

With an effort, I snapped out of it. *Dang, this guy was good.*

"Listen, wrinklepuss, I'm trying to *stop* the cheaters, not join 'em!" I turned and headed back out the door.

"If the need to cheat gets too strong, come see me," he called. "I'm always here to listen, Jet."

15

Stakeout & Potatoes

Sometimes a case ties your tail in knots. But sometimes Lady Luck smiles on you like a crocodile with a new set of choppers. This was one of those times. Not only did a strategy pop into my head on the walk back to class, but also I arrived just as the final bell rang.

Can't beat that for timing.

Natalie and I had a quick confab outside my door while waiting for the classroom to empty.

"Heya, Chet," she said. "I did some poking around during computer lab, and I think I found the Web site with the test answers."

"What was it?"

She smirked. "Cheatersalwaysprosper.com, of course."

"Did you get in?"

"Naw, couldn't crack it without the password."

I leaned on the wall. "Let's leave the cheating ring for tomorrow. Right now, we're gonna find out who framed Shirley."

I told her of my brainstorm.

She frowned. "I dunno, Chet. If you think it'll work..."

"Don't be a worry bird," I said. "Of course it'll work. And even if it doesn't, I've learned something to help us spot the culprit."

I repeated what Mr. Van Wrinkle had said about the reasons kids cheat.

Natalie cocked her head. "If that's true," she said, "our cheater should be Noah, Lacey, or Jack."

"How do you figure?"

Natalie counted off the reasons on her feather tips. "Pressure from the parents—that sounds like Noah and Lacey..."

"And Jackdaw Ripper is Mr. Flexible Morals," I said. "Well, whoever it was, we'll know pretty soon."

I peeked through the doorway. The last straggler had cleared the room. Mr. Ratnose strolled toward us.

"Here goes nothing," I said.

"But what if nobody tries to sneak in?" asked Natalie.

I clamped down my hat and scuttled up the wall.

"Then I've wasted a perfectly good stakeout. *Ssh*, here he comes!"

Mr. Ratnose stepped outside. I flattened myself against the wall above him.

"Oh, Mr. Ratnose?" said Natalie. "Can you answer something for me?"

He bent toward her. "Why of course, my dear." For some reason, Mr. Ratnose was always nicer to other teachers' students.

"Sir, I was wondering," Natalie said, as I eased around the doorframe behind my teacher's back. "I have a question about English that my teacher couldn't answer."

Mr. Ratnose smoothed his whiskers. "I'll certainly give it a try."

"Why is it that writers write, but fingers don't fing?"

"Eh?"

I was halfway through the door. He started to turn back toward me.

"Also," she said, "I've noticed that grocers don't groce and hammers don't ham. What's up with this language?"

Mr. Ratnose huffed. "Stop wasting my time, young lady." In one smooth move he shut and locked the door—just as I pulled my tail through. *Close call.*

My eyes adjusted to the dimness while my teacher's footsteps faded.

Natalie's voice came faintly through the door: "Good luck, partner."

"Thanks," I said. "Uh, *'fingers don't fing'*?"

"Hey, it worked, didn't it?"

I climbed down the wall and looked for a likely hiding place. Behind the aquarium or back by the sink? Ah, the supply cabinet. I slipped inside.

It was a tight fit amid the games and papers and such. Chalk dust tickled my nose and pencils poked me, but I closed the cabinet door, leaving a good-sized crack for spying.

Minutes lolled around like lazy sloths at naptime. I yawned silently and scratched my nose. Just when I thought this had been a really dumb idea, a soft *clickety-click* sounded at the classroom door.

I held my breath.

The door swung open. A dark figure stood framed in daylight. As he entered the room, I made out the mug of . . . Jackdaw Ripper! That sneak thief.

He strolled up the aisle, bold as brass, making straight for the teacher's desk. The magpie rummaged through the drawers and slipped something into a sack he was carrying.

Hah! I had him dead to rights. Just then, the chalk dust made my nose twitch. Pressure built behind my eyes. I pinched my nose and thought anti-sneezing thoughts.

Jack looked up at the supply cabinet. A smile creased his beak, and the shifty bird prowled toward my hiding place.

Uh-oh. I gripped the inside latch.

He stepped up to the cabinet and reached for the handle . . .

But just then, the front door rattled again!

Jack's gaze swept the room, settling on the aquarium. He fluttered over and took cover behind it.

When the door opened, another fowl stood in the doorway. What was this, a jailbird convention? The invader closed the door and tiptoed toward the teacher's desk, head down.

The bird opened a drawer and leafed through file folders. That's when I recognized her: the glamorous Lacey Vail! Was she a cheater, too? I bit my lip.

The dove drew out a file and scanned its contents. She frowned, replaced it, and started back toward the door. Then Lacey stopped by a student's desk and searched inside.

The urge to sneeze gripped me again. My nostrils trembled, and my face stretched like earwig taffy. *Down, boy!* I told myself.

The feeling passed. Mentally counting over from my own seat, I realized that Lacey Vail was searching her own brother's desk. But why?

Before I could figure it out, the dove shut the

desktop and scooted out the door. Then Jack slunk from behind the aquarium and followed her.

I slumped back against the shelves. Was everybody cheating in this class except me and Shirley? Lost in my thoughts, I heard a *thump,* which I assumed was Jack closing the door.

When a stray air current sent more chalk dust my way, I didn't fight it. I let rip with a loud "Ah-eh-ah-*TZOOOO!*"

The force of my sneeze blew the cabinet door open. I stepped out. And there, standing at his desk, was Mr. Ratnose.

"Exactly what," he snarled, "is the meaning of this?"

16

To Catch Some Grief

I held my palms out. "I can explain," I said. "I was on a stakeout and—"

Mr. Ratnose bore down on me, with teeth clenched and tail stiff as a frozen mantis burger.

"No need for explanations," he said. "I know exactly what you were doing."

I relaxed. "Good, 'cause this case—"

"You, sir, are a cheater!"

"Huh?"

A few kids had filed into the room. They hung back near the doorway and watched with the happy fascination of bystanders at a train wreck.

"I knew you were a so-so student," said Mr. Ratnose. "But I never thought you'd stoop so low as to steal test answers and sell them."

The other kids gasped.

"What?" I said. "But I didn't—"

"Hush!" he said. "Whip Van Wrinkle just told me about you. And now I find you've broken into the classroom. What am I to think?"

My tail curled. "I was just—"

"Not another word!" thundered the furious rat. He grabbed my collar and towed me over to my desk. "Mister," he said, "you are in a world of trouble. For starters, I'm giving you a full month of detention. And since I'm hosting detention today, you can begin right now."

He glared, daring me to speak.

For once, I kept my trap shut. Though the world felt wobblier than a macaroni footstool, I pulled my shoulders back and sat down.

Shirley parked herself beside me. She leaned over. "Chet?" she said.

I turned. "Yes, Shirley?"

"You are *so* fired."

"But—"

She tossed her head. "Don't speak to me again, you *cheater.*"

I sank my chin onto my hands. My tail drooped.

There I was: no freedom, no reputation, no client. No way could things get any worse.

Then Kitten Caboodle slid into a chair on my other side and broke out a notepad. "So tell me," she said. "How does this make you *feel*?"

I'll spare you the details of my time in the hoosegow (that's *jail* in private-eye talk) and how my dad took the news with such compassion. Let's just say I had to sleep standing up.

The next morning dawned bright and surly. I groused my way to school and met Natalie by the flagpole.

"Why the grump, chump?" she chirped. Early birds are *way* too cheerful.

"Just a month of detention and no more client," I said. "That's all."

"Oh, you mean this?" She held up a copy of the school paper.

The headline blared, CHEATING RING ROCKS SCHOOL—DETECTIVE SUSPECTED.

I snatched the newspaper and glanced at the story. How peachy. To add insult to injury, they'd used my school picture. I jammed the paper into my pocket.

"I'm toast in this town," I said.

"Extra crispy, with butter," Natalie agreed. "Now, how are we gonna turn this case around?"

"What do you mean? I'll go to class, do my detention, and try to forget all about it."

She *tut-tut*ted. "Don't be so negative. Say, I can cheer you up. How did—"

I cut her off. "No jokes. I'm throwing in the towel."

Natalie grabbed my shoulder. "That's not the Chet Gecko I know."

"Yeah? Maybe he wised up."

"Wisdom? Nah, that's not the Chet I know, either."

"Funny," I said. I sagged onto the flagpole base. "Partner, whoever's behind this has been three steps ahead of us from the beginning."

"So?" she said. "We always figure it out in the end."

"Not this time." I watched kids straggling, slow as the last hour of vacation, onto the school grounds. "I can't tell whether Jackdaw or Lacey framed Shirley—and Shirley fired us, anyway, so it doesn't matter."

Natalie sat beside me. "She'll come around," she said. "But meanwhile, we can work on the cheating ring, starting with that shifty raccoon Johnny Ringo."

"How?" I asked. "With those two wolverines around, we can't get close. And even if we could, Johnny Ringo's a tough nut to crack."

Natalie groomed her feathers. "To crack a tough nut, apply more pressure."

"Yeah, but the only one with that kind of weight is Principal Zero. And he'd never help us. We've got no proof."

"What if we gathered all our suspects together in the principal's office? Think we could squeeze the truth out of them?"

I turned to look at her. "But how could we get them there?"

"Ah-ah-ah," she said. "First, I've got to know: Are you on the case or off it?"

I tugged my hat low. "Partner," I said, "what's on your mind?"

Natalie raised an eyebrow. "I was thinking maybe . . . a lunch party."

17

The Feast That Launched
a Thousand Chips

By the time morning recess ended, Natalie and
I had set her plan in motion. With the Newt Broth-
ers as messengers, we passed out invitations to all the
suspects in the case.

You wonder, how could we expect everyone to
show up? Simple. We lied.

Lacey Vail approached me as I entered our classroom. "Am I really invited to an exclusive lunch
with Antone 'the Stone' Jones?" she asked.

Her eyes were deeper than a mole's root cellar,
and her breath was sweeter than peppermint moth-
flakes.

My throat went dry. "By...uh...special re-
quest," I said.

She clasped her perfect wings to her chest. "I

don't normally follow professional wrestling, you understand. But he's the dreamiest."

"Pretty dreamy." I fought a goofy grin that threatened to creep across my face.

"But I wasn't aware that you knew him."

"Oh, Antone and me, we're like *this*," I said. I figured my fib didn't count, since my fingers were already crossed.

The classes before lunch staggered by like a polka lesson with a three-legged dog. Although the threat of an afternoon test hung over us all, my gallery of suspects shimmered with delight.

Ah, the power of a celebrity invitation.

When the lunch bell sounded, I shot out the door like a lizard possessed. Even though the cafeteria ladies had promised to save us a table, the law of the jungle ruled the lunchroom. It was first-come, first-served, all the way.

I skidded up to the table with the RESERVED sign on it. Somehow, Olive Drabb had beaten me there. Sneaky critters, those mice.

"Olive, this says 'reserved.'"

"I can read, ya know," she droned. "But this is my usual table, and I says to myself, Olive, there's gotta be room at the inn for someone who's . . ."

Ay, that voice. I shook my head to keep from dropping into a standing nap. The lunchroom was filling up. No time to dicker.

"All right," I said. "You can stay."

"Gee, thanks, Chet, you—"

I held up a hand. "Don't speak. Just sit by the wall and keep your trap shut."

"Why, certainly, I—"

"Don't speak," I said. "I'm serious as a detention slip."

"Sure thing, it's—"

"You...no...speakee!"

Miraculously, she clammed up.

Natalie brought our trays, and I looked them over. Besides the usual overcooked veggies and potato-bug chips, the cafeteria ladies were serving cricket potpie, horsefly pizza, and for dessert, parasitic-lice pudding.

Perfect for our purposes.

We directed the suspects to their seats as they came. Nobody wanted to sit beside Johnny Ringo's wolverines, but we solved that by putting them between Johnny and Olive. That'd teach her to horn in on a party.

When everyone was settled, I stood.

"Thank you all for coming on such short notice," I said. "Has everyone got their food?"

As I scanned the table, I spotted a late, uninvited guest. The nosy kitty, Kitten Caboodle, had slipped onto the bench across from Olive. She returned my glare with an innocent smile.

"Bring on the Stone!" shouted Jackdaw.

The wolverines began chanting, "An-*tone,* An-*tone.*"

I held up a hand. "Now, now. It gives me great pleasure to announce . . ." Everyone looked up expectantly. ". . . That Antone won't be joining us today."

Their faces fell faster than steel-winged bumblebees.

"What?!" squawked Natalie. "No Antone?" She scooped up her cricket potpie, and as I stepped behind Noah Vail, she let fly.

Blorp!

The gooey mess landed smack in Noah's face.

"Why, you—" I muttered, snagging a pizza slice from his tray. I took a quick bite, Natalie ducked, and I flung the pizza right into Johnny Ringo's lap.

Noah and Johnny seethed like a pair of volcanoes. The wolverines looked ugly. (Of course, they always looked ugly.) The dove and the raccoon reached for their pudding, and at the last minute, Natalie and I dodged their throws.

Plonk! Ploop!

Parasitic-lice pudding dripped from the heads of Rimshot Binkley and Wolverine Two (or was it One?).

"Food fight!" I yelled.

From then on, animal nature took its course. Pizzas sailed, potpies wailed, and pudding plopped. Even the overcooked veggies vaulted into the act.

Our suspects slung food like a road-show version of *My Dinner with the Flying Karamazovs*. Everyone got into the fight—even Olive and Kitten.

Before the battle could infect the whole lunchroom, Natalie slipped away.

"I'll fraggle you for good, Gecko!" shouted Wolverine One (or was it Two?). He tossed a potpie my way. I didn't duck this time, but just opened wide.

Hey, a gecko's gotta eat.

Sooner than you'd think, we were wearing our lunches. The trays were bare. Johnny Ringo picked his up and started slogging toward me with murder in his eyes and pudding in his fur.

I crouched, ready to spring onto the wall.

FWEEEET!

A whistle blast cut through the din.

Beside our table stood a hefty tomcat with a bad attitude. Principal Zero. He didn't waste time; he didn't ask questions. He just said the five little words that warmed the cockles of my heart.

"Everybody, in my office. Now!"

18

Up the Creek without a Tattle

Principal Zero kept us cooling our heels in the waiting room, under the watchful eyes of his secretary, Maggie Crow, and Vice Principal Shrewer. Before we sat, Mrs. Crow spread paper towels on the seats.

"And don't drip on the carpet, if you know what's good for you," she squawked.

We squished into chairs, dripping pudding and pizza.

The spanking machine hummed in a corner. Nobody looked at it.

The ten of us food-slingers sat avoiding eye contact—Johnny Ringo and his two goons, me and my five classmates, and Kitten Caboodle, who was scribbling on her notepad. Actually, Johnny and his

wolverines didn't so much avoid my eyes as send daggers, spears, and laser blasts my way with each glance.

I sneered back, but it got old fast. Stuffing my
hands into my pockets, I discovered the school
newspaper Natalie had given me (plus a few gooey
crickets from the potpie, which I ate). To kill time, I
skimmed Kitten's story, CHEATING RING ROCKS
SCHOOL—DETECTIVE SUSPECTED.

"*'It's a sad, sad tale. My life is ruined,' cried Private
Eye Chet Gecko.*"

Her quote was a little off. Big surprise. What I'd
actually told her yesterday was, "Bug off or I'll tie
your tail into a knot."

But she was right. I had said the word *tail*.

I read on. Her story was surprisingly detailed.
Kitten mentioned that we'd interviewed Noah and
Lacey, and that we'd consulted Cool Beans.

She even included our encounter with Johnny
Ringo, complete with the wolverines' threat to
"bloop" Natalie and me. Did this reporter have radar
ears?

Bzzzt!

The buzzer derailed my train of thought.

"Yes, sir?" said Mrs. Crow to her intercom. Principal Zero's tinny voice snarled something. "Yes,
sir!" she responded.

The crow sauntered over and opened his office

door. "Time to face the music," she said. "Chester Gecko, you first."

I hate it when they use my full name.

Padding across the worn carpet, past the spanking machine, I went and stood before the principal's broad black desk. If I didn't handle this just right, I wouldn't be sitting down for weeks.

"Shut the door," he said.

I shut it. "I know this looks bad . . ."

"Bad?" he rumbled. "No. World hunger is bad. This is just annoying."

I started to breathe again.

"*Deeply* annoying," he said. "You've got ten seconds to explain how this happened. And if I don't like your answer, I'm taking away your private-eye badge and giving you another week of detention."

Dang. That badge cost me three comic books and seven cereal box tops.

"All right," I said. "The truth. I staged that fight."

"You what?"

"I did it to get everyone into your office."

Principal Zero's eyes narrowed. "*That's* your explanation?"

"There's more. One of those students is running a cheating ring. And one of them—maybe the same student—framed Shirley Chameleon to cover his tracks."

Mr. Zero studied me. His long tail twitched twice. He leaned onto his elbows.

"A bold claim," he said, "coming from someone who steals test answers."

"Ah, that. Actually, I was staking out the classroom to catch the cheater."

"I suppose you can prove all this?"

"With your help," I said.

Another long moment passed like a garden slug in steel boots. Then Principal Zero reached for his intercom button. "Mrs. Crow? Send them in."

I took a moment to lick some cheese off my hat brim. Mr. Zero frowned.

The other kids slouched into the office like death row inmates wearing their last meals. They stood in a rough line beside me.

Kitten raised her hand.

"Yes, Miss Caboodle?" said the principal.

"I don't belong here; I'm just a reporter."

"Then report *this*," said Principal Zero, slamming his fist onto the desktop. "Nobody leaves here until this question is answered: Who's behind all the cheating at Emerson Hicky?"

Nine pairs of eyes looked anywhere but at Principal Zero. Nine mouths kept quieter than King Tut's grandmummy.

I got the ball rolling. "Jackdaw Ripper," I said.

"Wasn't me," he rasped.

"When I was hiding in the supply closet of our classroom, I saw you break into Mr. Ratnose's desk and take something. Do you deny you were stealing the test key?"

Principal Zero cut in. "Remember, Ripper, I can smell a lie." He wasn't kidding; cats have a heckuva sniffer.

"I didn't steal no test key," said Jack.

"Come on. I saw—"

"He didn't," said Principal Zero. "But I'll want to know what he *did* steal—in a moment."

I paced past the magpie. "Then . . . his partner in crime stole the answers."

Jack frowned. "My 'partner in crime'?"

"Lacey Vail." I stopped in front of her. "You came in right after Jack, didn't you? You went through Mr. Ratnose's desk, then your brother's."

"Hey!" said Noah Vail. "You searched my desk?"

I waved a finger in Lacey's face. "You hid the test answers in Noah's desk, didn't you? Bad birdie. Were you trying to frame him like you did Shirley?"

"I beg your pardon," said Lacey in a voice like distant bells pealing. "I would never harm my brother, or Miss Chameleon."

Mr. Zero growled, "Answer the question."

Her eyes teared up. "I did break in, I admit. It was wrong. But I was afraid my brother was cheating, so I read the teacher's file on him and searched Noah's desk for the answer key."

"Oh," I said. "So . . . if it wasn't you . . . it was . . . *you!*" I turned and pointed a finger at Lacey's brother, Noah.

The dove ducked his head. "Yeah," he said softly, "I cheated."

Lacey cooed, a small sad sound.

"Sorry, sis," said Noah. "But you didn't find a test key in my desk, 'cause I used this instead." He fished a wristwatch from his T-shirt pocket.

A *wristwatch?* Rimshot Binkley had used a watch to cheat, too.

I tweaked Noah's beak. "So you framed Shirley, eh? You sorry little sneak."

"What are you, mental?" said Noah. "I just told you, I didn't use an answer key, so how could I frame Shirley with one?"

Duh. He was right, of course. I was missing something obvious. But what?

"Gecko," growled Principal Zero. "I'm losing patience. Either prove your case or prepare for the spanking machine."

A hubbub at the door interrupted us. "No. You

100

can't—" Maggie Crow was saying as Natalie slipped under her outstretched wing and into the room.

"Hold everything, ladies and gerbils," said my partner. "Give me a moment, and I think I can clear up this whole mess."

19

Grime and Punishment

Once the room settled down, Natalie Attired stepped up beside me. "Didn't think I'd let you have all the fun, did you?" she muttered.

At a nod from Mr. Zero, my partner faced the group. "So, what do we know?" she said. "We know the world is round. We know cheaters never prosper. We know if you laugh while drinking a milk shake, it spurts out your—"

"Miss Attired," rumbled Principal Zero, "do you have a point?"

"Aside from the one at the end of my beak?"

"Natalie . . . ," I hissed.

"Yes, I do," she said. "Here's my point. We've got the evidence we need to reveal the culprit. All we have to do is put it together."

The students exchanged looks and shifted nervously.

"For example," said Natalie, "we know that Jackdaw Ripper broke into Mr. Ratnose's desk and stole *something*. If it wasn't a test, what did he take?"

All eyes went to the magpie.

Jack hung his head. "I, uh, was ripping off school supplies. To sell."

Johnny Ringo and the wolverines glared at him. If looks were mail, theirs would've come from the dead-letter office.

A thought struck me. "Who were you selling to?" I asked.

Jack nodded at Johnny. "Him. That raccoon's been pushing hot goods all over campus."

"You lie!" shouted Johnny Ringo.

Mr. Zero sat up straighter. His claws sank into the scarred desktop. "Is this true, Ringo?" he growled.

The raccoon backed down. "Uh, yeah," he mumbled.

"And you," said Natalie, pointing at Rimshot Binkley. "We know that you cheated, too."

"Did n-no—" the rabbit began, until he saw the principal's face. "Um, okay, yeah."

Then I remembered something.

"Binkley," I said, "you used a watch to cheat." He nodded. "*And* you said you couldn't tell me who you bought it from, because 'Stripes' would kill you."

Rimshot Binkley gulped and nodded again.

I turned to the principal and opened my hands. "Then it's obvious who's behind the cheating ring. None other than that stripy character..." Natalie joined me in saying, "Johnny Ringo!"

Outrage flashed across the raccoon's face. "You gink-faced cheese-heads!" he said, clenching a fist.

Wolverine One muttered, "I shoulda blooped 'em yesterday."

"Sure, maybe I sold a few hot goods—" Johnny Ringo said.

Principal Zero stood.

"Okay," said Johnny, "a *lot* of hot goods. But I don't run a cheating ring."

The principal walked right up, eyeball-to-eyeball with him, and sniffed. "He's...telling the truth," said Mr. Zero.

I turned to Natalie. She shrugged, as confused as I was.

Then the wolverine's words sank in.

"Hang on," I said, walking over to Ringo's goons as I pieced it together. "You tried to bloop us yesterday, and the school paper reported it today."

"So what?" sneered Wolverine Two.

"If Kitten Caboodle quoted me wrong when I was right in front of her, how in the world did she quote you correctly when she wasn't even there?"

All faces turned to Kitten Caboodle. Mr. Zero crossed his thick arms.

"You know, I never noticed before," said Natalie, "but she's got stripes."

"Well, Miss Caboodle?" growled the principal.

Kitten looked around with her mismatched eyes and shrugged. "Hey, you gotta admit," she said, "it makes a great story."

20

That's Olive She Wrote

"A *story?*" Principal Zero rumbled. "You started a cheating ring on *my* campus just to have something to write about?"

Kitten Caboodle had the grace to look ashamed. "'Fraid so," she said.

"And you sent me those e-mails, just to keep me on the case," I said.

"Yup. Boy, you sure needed some big hints."

I rubbed my forehead. "Wait a minute, I don't get something. So what's the link between you and Mr. Racketycoon, here?"

Natalie stepped forward. "Don't you see, Chet? Johnny Ringo sold the watches, and Kitten's customers used 'em to store the test answers. They were in cahoots."

"Well, maybe just a half cahoot," said Kitten. "I got him the watches to sell, but I didn't tell him why."

"And then you sold your customers the password to your Web site so they could download test answers onto their watches," said Natalie. "Ingenious."

"Really?" I said.

Kitten smoothed her whiskers. "Thanks," she said. "It takes a computer nerd to appreciate a computer nerd."

Mr. Zero gripped her arm tightly. "Appreciate this. You are in very serious trouble, missy. I'm giving you double-Dutch detention, taking you off the school newspaper—"

"Nooo!" she wailed.

"—and having a talk with your parents about how to make sure you never even *consider* this kind of behavior again."

Kitten trembled. The other kids gave her a wide berth, as if her punishment might be catching.

"Chet and Natalie," said Principal Zero, "well done. For all your hard work, I'm giving you . . ."

"Free lunches?" I asked.

"Two days' detention—along with the rest of these troublemakers."

"But—"

"You wasted food; you littered school property," he said. "I'm letting you off easy. Don't push it."

I bit my lip. It didn't pay to argue with the grandmaster of detention.

Most of us trooped out of the office, leaving Kitten and my two dishonest classmates to their fate. I mused on the case. Breaking the cheating ring gave me a warm glow, but something was missing.

"Hey, Chet," said Natalie, as we headed down the hall with the others. "You okay?"

"It's just...I mean, we still don't know who framed Shirley."

A monotonous chuckle came from behind us. We turned.

"Um, that would be yours truly, don't ya know," said Olive.

"You?" I said.

"But why?" asked Natalie.

Olive Drabb scratched a pink ear. "Kitten's my very best friend," she droned. "And ya know that a friend in need is a friend indeed, or so they say."

I yawned and slapped myself, determined to hear her out. "Cut to the chase, Cheez Whiz. Why frame Shirley?"

"Kitten wanted a really dramatic story, with detectives and everything, ya know?"

Natalie's eyes were drooping, too. She said, *"Mm?"*

Olive blabbed on. "So I told her, 'Hey, Kitty-cat, if you wanna get the detective mixed up in it, just frame his girlfriend for cheating. She'll cry on his shoulder, and he'll...'"

But I didn't hear the rest of her story. Olive's hypnotic voice had lulled me off to dreamland.

A few minutes later, Natalie and I awoke on the concrete, refreshed, but with grooves worn into our cheeks. Everyone had returned to class, leaving us to nap in the hallway.

"That girl is some kind of boring," said Natalie.

"You can say that again." She started to open her mouth. "But don't."

We stood. I brushed potpie crumbs off my clothes. "Well..."

"Yeah...," she said.

"Guess I should get back to class and take that test."

Natalie groomed her wing. "I guess you should."

I stood there a moment longer.

"Tell me, Natalie. If you had one of those fancy watches and could get away with it, would you cheat on a test?"

Natalie raised an eyebrow. "Would you?"

We both chuckled and headed back to class. Some say that if a thing is worth having, it's worth a little cheating. But I say, for most things—a good friend, a satisfying case, a stack of Katydid Chunk bars—it's better to be true.

Will Chet suffer the Kiss of Doom?
Find out in
Give My Regrets to Broadway

Mr. Ratnose stepped to the edge of the stage and beckoned. "Chet Gecko," he said, "I'm going to do you a special favor."

"You're letting me out of performing in this dumb play?" I asked.

He got pricklier than a hedgehog's hug. "No," he huffed. "Our lead actor, Scott Frie, has disappeared."

My ears perked up. A missing person?

"You want me to find him, right?"

"Wrong again," said my teacher. "Shirley Chameleon, our leading lady, thinks you have talent—though I can't say why. I'd like you to take Scott's place."

"Me?"

"You."

"Thanks, but no thanks. I'm a detective, not an actor."

Mr. Ratnose crossed his arms. "Be that as it may. You will play the part, or you will write a fifty-page report on French classical theater."

He sure knew how to put the screws to a guy. The only thing I like less than looking foolish onstage is writing fifty-page reports (although math class and lima-bean pie are right up there).

I sighed. "Okay, I'll do it. Out of curiosity, what's the part?"

His black eyes sparkled, and a smile tweaked his ratty lips. "You'll play Omlet, Prince of Denver. You've got a dramatic duet with a ghost..."

"Swell," I said.

"A swashbuckling sword fight..."

"Excellent."

"And a romantic song with Azalea that ends in a kiss."

"That's—wait a minute! A *kiss!*?"

Mr. Ratnose nodded. "Yes, you fourth graders should be mature enough to handle it by now."

My stomach churned and tumbled like a dingo in a dryer. Sweat turned my palms into the Everglades.

"Wh-who plays Azalea?" I choked out.

"Why, Shirley, of course."

"*Gaa...*"

My mind spun. A lip-lock with Shirley Chameleon, Cootie Queen of the Universe? *Yikes!* In fact, *double* yikes.

"Well, what are you waiting for?" asked Mr. Ratnose. "Get up here and rehearse."

Right then, I decided. I would find Scott Frie before our play opened, or my name isn't Chet "Too Young to Be Smooched" Gecko.

Look for more mysteries from the Tattered Casebook of Chet Gecko in hardcover and paperback

Case #1 *The Chameleon Wore Chartreuse*

Some cases start rough, some cases start easy. This one started with a dame. (That's what we private eyes call a girl.) She was cute and green and scaly. She looked like trouble and smelled like . . . grasshoppers.

Shirley Chameleon came to me when her little brother, Billy, turned up missing. (I suspect she also came to spread cooties, but that's another story.) She turned on the tears. She promised me some stinkbug pie. I said I'd find the brat.

But when his trail led to a certain stinky-breathed, bad-tempered, jumbo-sized Gila monster, I thought I'd bitten off more than I could chew. Worse, I had to chew fast: If I didn't find Billy in time, it would be bye-bye, stinkbug pie.

Case #2 *The Mystery of Mr. Nice*

How would you know if some criminal mastermind tried to impersonate your principal? My first clue: He was nice to me.

This fiend tried everything—flattery, friendship, food—but he still couldn't keep me off the case. Natalie and I followed a trail of clues as thin as the cheese on a cafeteria hamburger. And we found a ring of corruption that went from the janitor right up to Mr. Big.

In the nick of time, we rescued Principal Zero and busted up the PTA meeting, putting a stop to the evil genius. And what thanks did we get? Just the usual. A cold handshake and a warm soda.

But that's all in a day's work for a private eye.

Case #3 *Farewell, My Lunchbag*

If danger is my business, then dinner is my passion. I'll take any case if the pay is right. And what pay could be better than Mothloaf Surprise?

At least that's what I thought. But in this particular case I bit off more than I could chew.

Cafeteria lady Mrs. Bagoong hired me to track down whoever was stealing her food supplies. The long, slimy trail led too close to my own backyard for comfort.

And much, much too close to my old archenemy, Jimmy "King" Cobra. Without the help of Natalie Attired and our school janitor, Maureen DeBree, I would've been gecko sushi.

Case #4 *The Big Nap*

My grades were lower than a salamander's slippers, and my bank account was trying to crawl under a duck's belly. So why did I take a case that didn't pay anything?

Put it this way: Would *you* stand by and watch some

evil power turn *your* classmates into hypnotized zombies? (If that wasn't just what normally happened to them in math class, I mean.)

My investigations revealed a plot meaner than a roomful of rhinos with diaper rash.

Someone at Emerson Hicky was using a sinister video game to put more and more students into la-la-land. And it was up to me to stop it, pronto—before that someone caught up with me, and I found myself taking the Big Nap.

Case #5 *The Hamster of the Baskervilles*

Elementary school is a wild place. But this was ridiculous.

Someone—or some*thing*—was tearing up Emerson Hicky. Classrooms were trashed. Walls were gnawed. Mysterious tunnels riddled the playground like worm chunks in a pan of earthworm lasagna.

But nobody could spot the culprit, let alone catch him.

I don't believe in the supernatural. My idea of voodoo is my mom's cockroach-ripple ice cream.

Then, a teacher reported seeing a monster on full-moon night, and I got the call.

At the end of a twisted trail of clues, I had to answer the burning question: Was it a vicious, supernatural were-hamster on the loose, or just another science-fair project gone wrong?

Case #6 *This Gum for Hire*

Never thought I'd see the day when one of my worst enemies would hire me for a case. Herman the Gila Monster was a sixth-grade hoodlum with a first-rate left hook. He told me someone was disappearing the football team, and he had to put a stop to it. *Big whoop.*

He told me he was being blamed for the kidnappings, and he had to clear his name. *Boo hoo.*

Then he said that I could either take the case and earn a nice reward, or have my face rearranged like a bargain-basement Picasso painted by a spastic chimp.

I took the case.

But before I could find the kidnapper, I had to go undercover. And that meant facing something that scared me worse than a chorus line of criminals in steel-toed boots: P.E. class.

Case #7 *The Malted Falcon*

It was tall, dark, and chocolatey—the stuff dreams are made of. It was a treat so titanic that nobody had been able to finish one single-handedly (or even single-mouthedly). It was the Malted Falcon.

How far would you go for the ultimate dessert? Somebody went too far, and that's where I came in.

The local sweets shop held a contest. The prize: a year's supply of free Malted Falcons. Some lucky kid scored the winning ticket. She brought it to school for show-and-tell.

But after she showed it, somebody swiped it. And no one would tell where it went.

Following a strong hunch and an even stronger sweet tooth, I tracked the ticket through a web of lies more tangled than a rattlesnake doing the rumba. But the time to claim the prize was fast approaching. Would the villain get the sweet treat—or his just desserts?

Case #10 *Murder, My Tweet*

Some things at school you can count on: Pop quizzes always pop up just after you've spent your study time studying comics; Chef's Surprise is always a surprise, but never a good one; and no matter how much you learn today, they always make you come back tomorrow.

But sometimes, Emerson Hicky amazes you. And just like finding a killer bee in a box of Earwig Puffs, you're left shocked, stung, and discombobulated.

Foul play struck at my school—that's nothing new. But then the finger of suspicion pointed straight at my favorite fowl: Natalie Attired. Framed as a blackmailer, my partner was booted out of Emerson Hicky quicker than a hop toad on a hot plate.

I tackled the case for free. Mess with my partner, mess with me.

Then things took a turn for the worse. Just when I thought I might clear her name, Natalie disappeared. And worser still, she left behind one clue: a reddish smear that looked kinda like cherry ladybug jam. This raised an ugly question: Was it murder, or something serious?